Incoming Call

James McHarg

Published by Troubled Skies Publishing, 2024.

This is a work of fiction. Similarities to real people, places, or events are entirely coincidental.

INCOMING CALL
First edition. 2015
Second edition. May 2, 2024.
Copyright © 2015 James McHarg.
Written by James McHarg.

To Helen - Always there for me.

To Nicole, Elizabeth, and Heather - My sincerest
gratitude for your invaluable input to the manuscript.

Chapter One

When the first call came in, Trey Laughlin had just beaten a man with a crowbar in a dark downtown alley. A numbing rain began falling shortly after midnight, which now drenched the towering hulk and cascaded over his dark clothing. Water poured from him in sheets, spilling onto the unconscious man lying at his feet, creating a blood-blackened stream that snaked into a nearby drain.

Shattered leg, busted shoulder. That should teach the deadbeat to pay his bills. Trey referred to all of his assigned targets as deadbeats. When it came to deadbeats, he had no interest in names, occupations, hobbies, or family status. If you were a deadbeat, it was his job to remind you to pay your bills. No matter who you were.

Trey, certain he powered the phone off, was startled when it came to life inside his pocket. As a meticulous professional he always took the precaution prior to a job and couldn't believe he forgot such an important detail. He jammed the crowbar under his arm, and with a gloved hand, fumbled around in his coat pocket as the phone continued to ring.

"Yeah. I hear ya, I *hear* ya."

When he extracted the phone, the display revealed an incoming call. "No shit. Must be why they call 'em smart phones." He held the phone to his face, a pugilist's face; wide, brawl-bashed nose, broad forehead, and a prominent chin slashed by a meandering scar resembling a dried-up riverbed. He squinted at the glowing screen as rain dripped from his eyelashes. There was no name, only a phone number. "616-565-7734, don't know who that is." He took the call anyway. "Who's this?"

An empty dial tone buzzed in his ear. "Same to you, pal," he shouted, holding the phone opposite his mouth. He stared once more at the unfamiliar number and wondered who would call him on *this* particular phone. After all, this was his work phone. Very few people knew the number, the most frequent caller being Tony Bavetta; the Mob Boss for the lower-east side, and his employer.

Gusts of wind funneled down the alley, driving the rain and late-October chill deeper into Trey's bones. It carried with it the pungent stench of a nearby dumpster, its vermin occupants rustling and clattering as they foraged for rotting morsels. *Rats. I hate 'em!*

That was his cue. Time to wrap up for the night. As soon as he dropped the phone into his pocket, it rang again. "Shit!" he said, exasperated. He yanked the phone from his pocket and glared at the screen. *Same number!* "Now you're really pissing me off!"

When he raised it to his face, a lifeless drone hummed in his ear. Whoever was calling was playing games with him and he didn't like it. Not one bit. His anger boiled as he attempted to retrieve the number from the call log. A blank screen shone up at him. "What's goin' on? It should be here." He searched again. Empty. "What's wrong with this thing?" he said, shaking the phone as if expecting to violently entice the needed information from it.

"Hey, you there!" The distant voice knifed through the pounding rain, jarring Trey from his preoccupation. His head jerked up and he squinted in the direction of the voice where the darkened alley spilled into the street.

The silhouetted figure was unmistakable. *It's a cop!*

He was so distracted by the cell phone, he didn't hear the car pull up, didn't even notice the approaching figure. *Where's your head at, Trey?*

"Stop where you are. What are you up to over there?" The lone cop's head bobbed and weaved like a prizefighter as he strained to see into the murkiness.

Trey, on the other hand, having spent plenty of time in dark alleys, had excellent night vision. This was *his* turf. He intimately knew every back alley, every street, every nook and cranny where a man could hide. With the lightning-quick precision of a sleight of hand magician, he slid the crowbar out from under his arm and tucked it securely into the back of his pants. He slowly hoisted his arms skyward.

The cop tilted his head to the right, dropped his chin, and clutched his lower-right shoulder while the other hand hovered anxiously over the holstered weapon. He muttered something inaudible, hushed and urgent, an electronic squeal, some hissing and clicking. Trey didn't have to hear the conversation. He just summoned backup using the radio microphone attached to the lapel of his jacket. Throughout the brief communication, the cop's eyes stayed fixed on the big man. Trey wondered if the cop hadn't noticed the unconscious deadbeat at his feet. He sure hoped so.

Just relax, be cool, he told himself. *No cop's gonna get the jump on Trey Laughlin. Not now. Not never.* He'd already come up with an escape plan.

"No worries, Officer. Just slipped out for a smoke." As Trey spoke, he waggled the cell phone, which he partially concealed in his left hand, hoping it would resemble a cigarette pack in the gloom. He slowly, calmly, inched forward until his large frame loomed between the uniformed man and the prone figure sprawled on the rain-soaked asphalt. "If we're all cool here, I can just be on my way."

"Freeze," the authoritative voice barked. "Not another step." The officer shuffled cautiously forward.

Just a little closer, Trey thought, *one more step...*

"No problem." When the cop drew his pistol, Trey's adrenaline spiked. "Whoa! Let's not do anything rash now." Trey stretched his arms further, feigning placid cooperation.

The din of the pouring rain engulfed the squalid alley, splashing down with the ferocity of a monsoon. Somewhere off in the distance, a siren wailed. Trey knew it called for him. His keen eyes could start to make out the advancing policeman's facial features. *He's young...and scared shitless.* As seconds lapsed, Trey became more and more convinced the cop hadn't seen the fallen man; at least, so far. He hoped he beat him well enough to remain unconscious. If he came to, it would spoil everything. He would only have one chance to carry out his plan, one shot, no more.

Behind the young cop, the plate-glass windows lining the desolate street were suddenly ablaze with the approaching cruiser's pulsing red lights. The siren's cry intensified. Backup had almost arrived.

"Toss the cigarettes. Down on your knees. Hands behind your head." With help imminent, the cop's bravado escalated. "Now!"

I've got to make my move. Trey's muscles went taut, a coiled snake ready to strike. He reached back, clasping the crowbar.

The pretend cigarette pack suddenly, noisily, announced an incoming call, giving away his ruse, surprising both men.

The gun jerked in the jittery cop's hand. At that moment, Trey thought he would catch a bullet right between the eyes. *Splat! Game over.*

Just then, the backup cruiser slid in behind the parked black-and-white, tires splashing and siren fading. The young police officer made a rookie mistake. He took his eyes off Trey, just for a split-second, and glanced back at the new arrival.

It was all the time Trey needed. He yanked the crowbar from the back of his pants, and with the skill of a carnival knife-thrower, tossed it at the legs of the distracted cop.

Without hesitation, Trey wheeled around and bolted into the dark embrace of the alley. Behind him, another wail pierced the rain-washed night. This time it wasn't a siren.

Chapter Two

As the personal enforcer for a powerful Mob Boss, Trey had three key responsibilities, what he liked to call "the three B's": bouncer, bodyguard, and most importantly, bill collector. "It's everyone's responsibility to pay their bills," Tony Bavetta told him in his deep baritone, "and when they don't, I like to send a message to remind them they shouldn't shirk those responsibilities. That's where you come in, Big Guy."

That was three years ago, and in that time, Trey sent a lot of "messages". At first, a subtle reminder was all that was needed – Trey's gargantuan stature usually resulted in immediate compliance. Sometimes, when the initial reminder was conveniently forgotten, a second visit with a crowbar became necessary. Trey never, *ever*, had to visit a three-peat deadbeat. He was very good at jogging memories.

There were periods of time when nothing was required of him and Trey liked that the least about the job. This was one of those times. Over the three days that followed his brush with the cop in the alley, Trey experienced a lull and whiled away his time with other distractions. As usual, he spent an abundance of time at Tony Bavetta's nightclub, Vertigo Palace. His favorite barmaid, Maggie Valente, worked the night shift. A night-owl by nature, he often stayed until closing, participating in the occasional backroom poker game, listening to the idle chatter of fellow barflies, and taking in the nightly entertainment. Though, his favorite distraction by a long shot was Maggie Valente. Trey sat at the bar for hours and told Maggie things he could tell no one else.

It was approaching two-thirty on a Saturday morning, the entertainment had wrapped up for the night, and Ol' Blues Eyes' soulful crooning drifted melodically from the jukebox. At this late hour, sparse few patrons remained at the bar. The oak bar top was just scrubbed for the night, smelling of pine and shimmering like the Vegas Strip under the rainbow glow of the bar lights.

Trey, sullen after a losing effort at poker, took a seat at the bar.

"Hey there, huge, dark, and handsome," Maggie playfully greeted, already drawing him a pint. "What's up? You've been quiet all night. Even more than usual, I mean." She slid the froth-topped glass to him. It stopped as if by command, directly in front of him.

Trey didn't respond, preoccupied with the cell phone clutched in his palm.

Maggie persisted, "Wow, sulky *and* quiet. What happened, little boy? Someone steal your pony?"

Trey looked up from his lap, and in spite of his mood, smiled. "No...nobody stole my pony." He could lose himself in Maggie's sweet magnolia scent, could stare into her Hollywood starlet eyes for hours, if Maggie would let him. Her voice, her sultry, gravelly voice, could make any man stop in his tracks to listen. Around this joint, maybe even a woman or two. Trey often told her she could read Edgar Allen Poe and somehow make him sound sexy. "Got some work stuff on my mind. Had a close call, is all."

"You okay?"

"I'm cool. Just let myself get distracted for a sec." His attention returned to his lap.

"You expecting a call? You're looking at that phone like the Godfather himself is about to call."

"Uh, no," he said, looking up distractedly, "it's turned off, matter of fact."

"Well, why don't you turn it *on* then?"

"No," he blurted. "I mean, I'm gonna put it away now." He plopped it into his shirt pocket and gulped a mouthful of beer.

"You *sure* you're okay, Trey?" She always called him Trey when the conversation turned serious. "You seem awfully distracted by that phone of yours."

"I said I'm cool," he snapped. Then, regretting his outburst, "Hey, Maggie, I'm sorry. Didn't mean nothin' by that. We're good, okay?"

Maggie gave him an uncertain stare. "Yeah, we're good."

Trey peered into her beautiful, auburn eyes, became lost in them for a moment, and finally said, "Do me a favor. Could you maybe not say anything to Mister Bavetta? About my close call, I mean. He doesn't need to know about that. It's just a blip on the radar. Nothin' I wanna trouble the Boss with."

"No worries. Your secret is safe with me. Another beer?" she asked, glancing at his empty glass.

"Yeah."

She poured a fresh pint.

Sinatra's smooth voice faded to silence and Rod Stewart's throaty vocals cut in, imploring *Maggie May* to wake up so he could get something off his chest.

Maggie's face flushed. "Aw, that's sweet. You choose that one for me?" As soon as she asked the question, a cell phone rang a few stools over. Trey flinched and anxiously clutched his shirt pocket.

An awkward moment of silence passed between them until, finally, he looked up at Maggie, embarrassed. "Goddammit can't get no peace anywhere these days without some damn phone blaring." He downed the rest of the beer and stood up, hovering briefly. "Well, I better go. It's getting late. Goodnight, Maggie. See you tomorrow."

"Sure thing. You take care of yourself, all right?"

Maggie's tone was much too motherly for his liking and he shot her a disapproving glance. He then turned and stalked away.

PERPLEXED, MAGGIE WATCHED Trey leave. Her concern only deepened at seeing Trey dig the phone from his pocket just before disappearing through the exit.

What's gotten into Trey, she wondered, *and what's up with the phone?* He seemed out-of-sorts all night. This she found highly unusual because, as far as she was concerned, his cool, calm demeanor had yet to be matched by anyone. In the year she knew Trey, she saw him stare down groups of men – troublemaker types – without batting an eye. Saw him easily dispense with drunks who became aggressively flirtatious toward her without as much as a quiver. This new, jittery Trey was an anomaly, as foreign to her as wearing white socks with Stiletto heels.

When he jumped at the sound of the ringing phone, she dared not acknowledge her awareness of it. At first, she was so unsettled by his nervousness, she questioned if she saw it at all.

Though it seemed too incredible to even consider, she had to ask herself: *What could Trey Laughlin possibly be afraid of?*

She removed the empty glass, placed it in the bin for washing, and gave the bar a final wipe. When she turned toward the small sink, Maggie realized she wasn't alone.

At the far end of the bar, nearly tucked out of sight, a well-attired, slender-built man spun around on his stool, turning his back to her, and pressed a phone to his ear. Had she seen him here before? He looked familiar, and she was quite good with faces, but with his back turned, her view was limited.

Curious, she sauntered closer, and busily went about arranging the wine glasses dangling from the overhead rack, all the while keeping her attention on the stranger. The man spoke with a refined French accent, and in a soft whisper, she heard him say, "*Oui*, he has departed. Do you wish me to follow? *Non?* Until tomorrow, then."

When the conversation ended, he spun back around. He had a long, thin face: a slender, arching nose, slightly askew and black, oil-slicked hair. What unsettled her most, though, were his cold and malevolent eyes, which bore into her like a hungry lion sizing up its next meal. She tensed, but managed to raise the corners of her mouth in a weighted smile.

He smiled back, but the eyes stayed the same. "*Bonsoir, Mademoiselle,*" he said, raising hand to temple and flipping a two-fingered salute. With a flourish reminiscent of royalty, he stood, turned, and strutted to the door. Long after he left, the scent of his expensive cologne lingered. To Maggie it smelled like trouble.

Chapter Three

The long-awaited call finally came in. It was so long since his work phone rang Trey could barely contain his excitement at hearing the Boss's voice.

According to Mister Bavetta, his newly assigned target had an affinity for gambling and the high-life, neither of which he could afford. After becoming delinquent on numerous gambling debts, the man switched allegiances from Vertigo Palace to a new, swanky club, The Macambo, in this highbrow part of town.

"If the man has enough cash to spread around *that* part of town," Bavetta told him, annoyance embedded in his tone, "he most certainly has enough cash to pay his debts." To expedite tracking, Bavetta provided the man's name and cursory description, but as always, left the subtle details to his enforcer.

To get a feel for his routine, Trey shadowed the deadbeat for a few days and came to the discovery that on Tuesday's and Wednesday's he spent a few hours gambling at The Macambo, and then left sharply at one-thirty in the morning.

It was now 1:22 a.m.

The November night air had teeth, the wind biting at the exposed flesh of his face. Trey pressed his back against the brick wall as he huddled at the mouth of an alleyway. He strategically selected this particular alley because it was poorly lit and the wall contained a setback, which easily hid his large frame. He also learned his target would walk right by this very alley on his way home from the club. Best of all, he discovered the deadbeat had one habit which played right into his plans. He liked to whistle, show tunes, no less. So he would know exactly when the man drew near. It was perfect. *After tonight, the deadbeat won't be whistling Dixie for quite a while*, thought Trey.

He flipped up the collar of his black bomber jacket, then fumbled around in his hip pocket and extracted the cell phone. *Powered off. Good.* He returned it to his pocket. It was the third time he checked the phone in the last hour.

A few minutes later, the high-pitched, melodic sound he patiently waited for caught his attention. The whistling drew near, echoing along the deserted corridor, piercing the silence with its haunting intonation, like a far-off loon's cry at dusk. Trey clenched his gloved hands expectantly.

Almost here, thought Trey, *just a few more steps.* As always, a deep calm overtook him. He became as still and focused as a jungle cat ready to pounce, his unsuspecting prey oblivious to its fate. His ears were attuned to any sound that might indicate danger. Aborting the attack was always an option if he felt it wasn't safe. Better to remain a ghost in the shadows than to risk exposure or capture. As long as his presence remained unknown, another opportunity would always present itself. So far, he detected nothing to make him wary.

The deadbeat was a step or two away from the alley where Trey lurked, an arms-reach away from any passerby. His plan was simple: grab him, cover his mouth, and drag him deep into the shadows of the alley. From there, he would be free to pass along Mister Bavetta's message undisturbed.

At that very second, two events occurred simultaneously: the deadbeat strolled into Trey's line of sight, and the cell phone in Trey's pocket trilled.

The deadbeat's whistle stuck in his throat. His head spun toward Trey. The man gaped at the skulking giant in the shadows.

For the first time in Tony Bavetta's employ, Trey froze. The phone's disruptive clamor grew louder until it reached an ear-splitting pitch.

The two men stared at each other, neither able to move. A glint of fear mixed with familiarity flashed in the deadbeat's eyes and he darted off with the swiftness of a sprinter leaving the starting blocks.

"Help! Police! Help me! I'm being attacked!" the panicked man screamed, his words echoing off buildings and reverberating through the deserted neighborhood. Trey wanted to take up the chase, but was held fast by shock and dismay. Already, lights in nearby apartment windows flashed on and he knew it was too late. He failed. *What am I gonna tell the Boss? He doesn't like failure.*

The relentless ringing finally jolted him from the stupor. Now he was furious. He snatched the phone from his pocket. The familiar number burned into his retinas. He pressed the phone to his ear. "What do you want from me? Who *is* this?" As he screamed into the phone, more lights popped on, and soon, silhouetted figures materialized in nearby windows. He didn't care. Blind rage took hold and Trey was suddenly oblivious to his surroundings.

The device hissed, hummed, and crackled, but he heard no voice. An electronic squeal, like feedback from a powerful guitar amp, assaulted his eardrum and he jerked the phone away, grimacing.

Holding the phone to his lips, he continued, "Don't know who you are, but I'm gonna find out. When I do, you're dead meat. Got it! Dead meat!" The squealing continued like a million screams resounding inside his head, and then, finally, silence.

From a second-floor window, a distant voice cried out, "Hey, pal! Keep it down out there. Don't make me call the cops. Jesus! People are trying to sleep here!"

Trey glanced toward the source of the angry voice and then caught sight of the deadbeat just as he disappeared around a distant corner. It would be pointless to pursue him, and he now realized if he lingered any longer in this neighborhood, he would be putting himself in danger. His last close call with the cops was one too many.

He returned his attention to the silent phone, attempting to activate it without success. It was powered off. *That doesn't make sense. What's going on? Maybe it's broke. Yeah, that's it. These damn gadgets do funny things sometimes. Maybe I should get a new one.* Having received the phone from Mister Bavetta, he knew he'd have a hard time explaining why he needed another. The Boss liked thoroughness, discretion, and professionalism. This was why he hired Trey for such a highly regarded – and highly coveted – job. He already had some explaining to do after tonight's failed assignment. Trey knew locating the target now would prove more difficult. Tony Bavetta would not take that news lightly.

For the first time in his adult life, he felt an emotion utterly foreign to him: fear. He didn't like the feeling. Not one bit. It gnawed at his belly and washed over him like a cold shower. A car whisked past, startling him. He turned and strode down the alley into the safety of blanketing darkness.

Trey powered up the phone, and although he had no previous success, he opened the call log in hopes the number might be saved. Surprisingly, this time it was there. 616-565-7734 glowed up at him. Calling the number seemed like a good idea, but after four static-filled responses, it became obvious making contact wasn't going to be *that* easy. He felt the warm flush of anger radiate under his collar. It wouldn't be too difficult to put a trace on the number, he supposed. He had acquaintances that could assist him, people with expertise in electronic tracking, telephone surveillance, and such. He was determined to discover the caller's identity so he could pay him a little visit. With his trusty crowbar, of course.

"Like to see him try to use a phone with porridge for fingers," he muttered, powering down the cell. Imagining a confrontation with the infuriating caller improved his mood; a feeling cut short when the phone sprang to life in the palm of his hand. The electronic bleating rocked his nerves with such ferocity he almost dropped the phone. The display lit up with astonishing brilliance, illuminating his shocked face, stabbing at his eyes.

"What the..." He had enough, his gut tightening into a knot of unbridled rage. Fury and frustration no longer containable, he snapped and pitched the phone. It smashed against the jagged brick of the alley wall, showering the ground with dozens of fragments of plastic, glass, and bits of electronics.

The big man stood quietly in the dark alley, chest heaving, fists clenching, and eyes popping, as he stared in disbelief at the hopelessly shattered phone. As seconds ticked by and some semblance of reason returned, Trey considered the dire consequences of his actions.

"Shit," he uttered dismally.

Chapter Four

As a young girl standing on the stone steps, dwarfed by the towering granite arches, the grand mahogany doors yawning open before her, Maggie Valente viewed the *Basilica di Santa Maria* as more than just a church. When witnessed through the imagination-fueled eyes of a twelve-year-old, it evoked images of an ancient Gothic castle, all at once inspiring awe and inducing fear. The interior served only to enhance her childhood sense of wonder and trepidation. Now, as she stood inside the entryway of this magnificent piece of architecture some twenty years later, those same feelings swept her up like a crushing wave.

The vaulted ceiling appeared to stretch to the stratosphere, becoming one with the heavens. Numerous statues of religious figures lined the gilded walls, positioned in such a manner as if to scrutinize each new arrival. Stained glass windows, exquisite in design and vibrant in color, bathed the church in a kaleidoscopic shimmer in the afternoon sunlight.

At this time of day the church was empty, and as she scanned the expanse of it open-mouthed, feeling all of twelve years old once again, she uttered, "Jeezuz…" Perched above her, as if descending from the heavens, a stone statue of the *Beata Virgine Maria* seemed to glare down upon her. "Oops. Sorry, Mary," she said, covering her mouth. "I promise I won't use the Lord's name in vain again. Strike me dead if I do."

She walked these aisles so long ago, but the memories rushed back to her as if they happened only yesterday. Her father brought her here many times as a child. It was their escape from the hardness of life and from the dangers that befell their family. Over time, she grew to adore the church visits with her dad and bask in the warmth of their bond. Father and daughter would sit or kneel quietly in a pew, hand-in-hand, listening to the service and praying silently. Young Maggie didn't pray for herself though, she prayed for her father and mother. Soon after those most cherished times, at the tender age of twelve, innocence was lost, faith decimated, and a young girl's life forever changed. *She* was forever changed. When it came to answering her prayers, God had failed her, and she had not set foot in a church since.

Maggie, still at the back of the church, feet cemented to the floor, transfixed by horrific memories, finally managed to gather her courage and turn to her left. Gliding along the back row, she headed toward the north wall, turned right, walking briskly along the side aisle, until she arrived at a small room located at the halfway point. She entered the room. The air felt stale here, almost stifling, and the lighting, vapid at best. She approached the only piece of furniture in the room, a confessional booth made of dark-stained oak.

When she flung back the heavy curtain, her heart did a drum roll. "Jesus, it's tiny," she muttered, and then realized she just broke her promise to Mary. *Hope this place is grounded against lightning strikes,* she thought, scanning overhead.

Taking a calming breath, she eased herself onto the wooden bench and awkwardly performed the sign of the cross. She sat quietly for a moment, then said, "Bless me Father for I have sinned." A one-foot square shuttered opening separated her from whoever occupied the other side. The horizontal slats rotated partially open, revealing intermittent facial features of an older man: thick, gray eyebrows, dark eyes staring forward and away from her, and weathered, well-bronzed skin.

The eyes turned toward her. They were intense and moist, as if touched by tears. "*Mia Bambina*. It is so good to see you." The man spoke softly, with a slight Italian accent.

"It's good to see you, too, Uncle. It's been too long. I fear I'm not so much your *bambina* anymore. I've changed, you know. I had to grow up fast, and I'm not as sweet as you might remember." Maggie wanted to reach through the blinds and touch her uncle's face, feel his warmth, his love, but she couldn't. There wasn't much time and too much was at stake.

"Uncle...I've got this uneasy feeling there's something brewing at Vertigo Palace. I don't know what exactly, but I've seen a man around the club. Well dressed, kind of snooty looking, creepy too. He's definitely not local. He speaks with a French accent. You know him?"

"I might. Does this complicate things?"

"Maybe, I don't know. There's something else I need to tell you...Wait, what's that?" Thinking she may have heard something, she pulled back the curtain and peered through the slivered opening. All seemed quiet. "Is Father Iganzio here?" she asked nervously.

"Yes, he's here."

"Does he know you're here?"

"He knows, but he'll leave us be for a few minutes. He's a very good friend of mine." From behind the confessional's dividing wall, paper rustled. "We don't have much time, *Mia Bambina*.

We must act quickly and be on our way as soon as possible. Are you certain you weren't followed?"

Maggie, annoyed by the question, said, "I'm *most* certain. There's no reason to be concerned. I've learned much through the years. You placed me in very good hands."

"Good." A letter-sized envelope, bulging in the middle, poked through a crack in the veins. "I want you to take this." When Maggie took hold, the weight of it pressed heavily against her palm.

"I have no time to explain, but you will see there is a note inside. It will have all the information you will need. Keep the contents safe and hidden. I must go. I am expected elsewhere. Be careful. *Ti amo, Mia Bambina.*"

"I love you, too, Uncle."

The shutter flipped shut, and Maggie *felt* rather than saw her uncle leave. Alone in the confessional, she was overcome by emptiness, a feeling of loss. It burned in the pit of her stomach and choked the back of her throat. She was once again left wondering if she made the right decision. She left so much behind to come here, but stubbornly held to the belief the sacrifice was necessary.

She took one more peek behind the curtain, and when satisfied she was alone, delicately, quietly, peeled the envelope open. She dug inside and extracted the weighty object: a loaded Smith & Wesson .38 Chief's Special. She fired such a weapon before at a gun range and became familiar with its handling.

As for the note, she would read it later. She needed to get out of this place. The coffin-like booth, the stuffy room, even the church itself, despite its colossal dimensions, began to close in around her. She suddenly felt smothered. She stuffed the gun, envelope, and note in her purse and made a speedy exit.

Once outside, Maggie paused on the steps to catch her breath. When she regained her composure, she realized, in her haste, she failed to report an important matter to Uncle: Trey Laughlin.

Chapter Five

Trey dawdled at the bottom of the stairs and stared up at Tony Bavetta's office. A source of great pride to Bavetta, the expansive room was built atop the AADCO Building on the thirty-third floor. A two-way mirror, strategically installed on the east-facing wall, allowed complete oversight of Vertigo Palace on the floor below while maintaining the viewer's privacy and security from within. On Bavetta's strict orders it was constructed from bulletproof glass. To further satisfy the Mob Boss's justifiable paranoia, the walls were lined with impenetrable steel. More than just an office, it was a fortified safe room.

A sour-faced man, who would have otherwise appeared large if he weren't standing alongside Trey, nodded toward the stairs and impatiently nudged him forward.

Trey shot him a stinging glare. "Yeah, yeah, I'm goin'." He climbed the dimly lit stairs, something he hadn't done in days, took a deep breath, and knocked on the door.

"Enter," the muffled voice commanded.

Wary, he fanned open the door and found Tony Bavetta seated at his large desk with pen in hand, poring over paperwork. Trey waited patiently for an invitation to enter, but Mister Bavetta ignored his presence.

Though the Mob Boss was a modern man, the office decor was a throwback to the 1930's gangster era, with rich, mahogany furnishings, crimson, deep-pile carpeting, desk the size of a billiard table, and accompanying high back, leather chair. One particular piece in the room, and the most unusual, always attracted Trey's eye first. It was an antique roulette wheel, which was wall-mounted and motorized to perpetually spin. Trey found it somewhat distracting, but Tony Bavetta apparently spent a good sum of money on the customization and no one dared speak negatively of it.

"Hi, Boss," Trey said sheepishly, still in the doorway.

Bavetta raised a halting hand, clearly not yet ready, or willing, to greet his visitor.

Trey remained silent, watching the roulette wheel rotate hypnotically. Bavetta once told him he acquired the prized piece over twenty years ago from a former Vegas competitor. When Tony Bavetta strategically took over the neighboring casino, the man's business crashed like the 1930's stock market. As for the wheel's former owner, he owed too much money to too many mobsters and mysteriously disappeared. Trey had a feeling the man's disappearance was a mystery to all but the Boss.

Trey never really understood the significance of the roulette wheel, nor did he understand the Boss's fixation with it. A close associate of Tony Bavetta's once told Trey that soon after acquiring the wheel, the ambitious young gangster rocketed to a position of power within the Mob.

At last, Bavetta threw down his pen, rubbed his eyes, sighed heavily, stood, and smiled over at his guest. He was of below-average height, solidly built, round-faced with thinning black hair. Impeccably dressed in a dark Giorgio Armani suit and pearl-white shirt, he reminded Trey of a modern day Al Capone. His smile, as disconcerting as it was genuine, made a lasting impression upon anyone in its proximity. Those who really knew Tony Bavetta weren't fooled by the smile though. They knew hidden behind it lurked a man as vicious as a crocodile.

"Come in, Big Guy. Sorry to keep you waiting. I'm glad you could make it. *Finally*."

Trey shuffled uncomfortably at hearing the word "finally". It was three days since his failed job and he knew the Boss was pissed. He had some explaining to do and despite the passing of time, still wasn't sure how he would account for his actions. His plan was simple: wing it.

"Come in. Come in. Don't be a stranger." Although Bavetta waved a welcoming hand, the smile vanished and his face transformed into a portrait of anger. "Please. Sit."

Trey remained silent and sat across from Bavetta, the well-polished desk sprawling between them. The Mob Boss hovered for a few seconds, glowering down at Trey, and finally settled comfortably into the lush chair.

"Sorry to send one of the boys to get you, but it seems that you've been incommunicado for a few days. Manny treated you well, I trust?"

"Yeah, fine"

"You know I don't like it when I can't contact my people. Makes me wonder what they're up to." He removed a fresh Cuban cigar from an ornate wooden box, clipped the end of it, and lit it. Puffing hard, smoke billowing, he asked, "What happened?"

"Uh, I'm sorry, Mister Bavetta. I was gonna call you. I really was. But–"

"Stop sputtering and just spit it out. I want to know how it was you messed up so badly that you allowed that little piece of shit to get away. Now I'll probably *never* see my money."

Trey pondered what to say next, but as anxiety mounted, clarity of thought became an uphill battle. Verbal confrontations were not his strong suit. He much preferred the physical variety. "I was interrupted."

"*How* were you interrupted? Come on, I'm losing patience here." He took another puff, blew another smoke cloud, this time in Trey's direction.

Trey continued, unfazed by the sickly-sweet haze of cigar smoke. "It was my phone. My phone rang. Just like that. It scared him off. I always power it off before a job. Honest. Guess I forgot." Trey shifted his large frame in the leather chair.

"You *forgot?*" Bavetta sucked in more smoke, breathing it out as he spoke. "I suppose you *forgot* to call me when the job went sour."

"No. I mean, I was gonna call, wanted to call, but the phone broke. Please, it won't happen again. Not ever again. I swear."

Bavetta continued to puff while scowling at Trey for a full minute as the big man sat quietly, fighting the urge to fidget. The heavy silence made Trey want to explain further, but his memory of the events in the alley remained foggy. Even after three days of reflection, it defied a simple explanation; at least a rational one. In the end, anything he said now would only sound like a lie. He convinced himself that no explanation would satisfy the Boss at this point.

Finally, Bavetta broke the silence. "Tell you what. Let's just call it water under the bridge, shall we? You've been one of my best enforcers, and I like you. I really do. You're more than just an employee. You're like family to me. I have an idea how you can make it up to me."

Trey leaned forward in the chair; relieved the interrogation was over, eager to move on. "I sure wanna make it up to you."

"Well then, sounds like you're ready for another job. No screw-ups this time. This is an important job, and if you prove to me you can handle it, I'll forget about past indiscretions."

Trey, uncertain as to what "indiscretions" meant, was smart enough to know it had something to do with screwing up. "Yeah, I'm ready, anything at all. Just name it."

The Mob Boss leaned forward and rested on one elbow, his eyes narrowing. "I've told you before that my son has been nothing but a disappointment to me. Marco's been a thorn in my side since puberty. His mother treated him like a delicate flower all his life, and that's exactly what he's turned into, a goddamn pansy. You, Big Guy, are more of a man than he'll ever be. Now he's pushed me too far. I have a source that told me he's hooked up with some slut. How do I know she's a slut?"

Trey shook his head.

"I know, because she's the daughter of *Dino Pentangelo!*" Bavetta's teeth clenched through tight lips. "Like all Pentangelo women, you can bet she's slept with more men than bed bugs at a sleazy motel."

The Bavetta-Pentangelo feud erupted two decades prior to Trey's association with the Mob Boss, so only whispered stories were ever relayed to him. Stories of a bitter, prolonged turf war over gambling profits in the lower-east side. It was horrific and devastating to both sides. There was as much spilled blood as bad blood between the two families. Over the years, the war subsided, although seething hatred still bubbled below the surface like magma trapped inside a dormant volcano.

Trey's eyes lit up. "So, you want me to mess him up?" He never met the younger Bavetta, but was appalled to hear the kid would treat his father so disrespectfully. Maybe a little roughing up would do the spoiled brat a world of good.

"Mess him up? No, I don't think you get it. My son is seeing the daughter of Dino Pentangelo; a murderous monster that killed members of my family. This isn't some childish prank or some foolish, rebellious behavior. This is the ultimate humiliation, the ultimate betrayal!" Bavetta's deep voice rumbled like thunder. "I've had it with him. As far as I'm concerned, he's no longer my son. No longer part of the Bavetta family!" He hammered the desk with his fist. Surrounding items quivered with the force of the blow.

Although Trey witnessed the Boss's fury before, he never saw him *this* angry.

Bavetta stared down at his clenched fist for a moment. A choking silence filled the room, and Trey swallowed hard. When he raised his head up to meet Trey's gaze, a blend of anger, disgust, and disappointment showed in the Boss's eyes. "What I want you to do – what I'm ordering you to do – is kill him. I want my son dead." His tone suddenly turned business-like; exuding no more emotion than if he just asked Trey to clean his pool.

Trey went numb.

Bavetta slid a hand under the desk, extracted a brand new phone and a handwritten note from a small recess, and slid them across the desktop. "I want you to call me as soon as it's done."

He sat back and crossed his arms. Behind the stoic mask, pain lurked, darkening Bavetta's eyes like storm clouds.

Trey opened his mouth to respond, but the words *kill* and *dead* rumbled through his brain, obliterating all other thoughts. Killing was against his credo, but how could he tell the Boss that he couldn't – *wouldn't* – kill anyone? "I've never done *that* before, never killed a man. It's kind of a personal code of mine."

"I'm not asking. You screwed up, and screwed up big. You owe me. Now, I'm collecting. Don't disappoint me like...*him*." The father couldn't even utter the name of his own son. He pointed at the cell phone. "I'm the only one who knows that phone number. Don't give it out to anyone. You keep it turned off until the job is done. Then, you call me. Is that clear? And for God's sake don't break it." Bavetta reached into the recessed compartment and retrieved another object: a small-caliber pistol. "I keep this handy...just in case. A man in my position can never be too careful. Here, you take it. It'll do the job." He extended the gun toward Trey.

"No. No guns," Trey blurted. "Don't like 'em. Don't use 'em. Only crowbars." He was horrified and didn't know what else to say. He was left with no alternative. There was no way he could turn down this job.

"Crowbars? Hmmm...sounds painful," Bavetta said, thoughtfully rubbing his chin. He slipped the gun back into the cubbyhole.

"How soon?" Trey asked.

"Tonight."

Trey's normally rock-solid stomach lurched.

"I called Marco earlier and asked him to meet me at my warehouse by the docks at ten. All the details you'll need are in the note. I told him we needed to talk. You know, to patch things up. Just father and son, no one else." His eyes were hallow, his voice emotionless. "He's pretty punctual. I want you to be there to greet him. When it's done, you call me. Don't mess this one up. Don't disappoint me again. Now, I've got work to do." Bavetta nodded toward the door.

"Sure thing. You won't be disappointed. I promise." Gut still reeling, Trey gathered up the phone and note, and hurried to the exit.

TONY BAVETTA WAITED until his enforcer shut the door behind him. He then scribbled another note, and picked up the phone. "Manny, tell the Frenchman I want to see him in my office now. Tell him to be discreet. I don't want anyone to see him."

Two minutes later, a tall man of slight build, wearing a dark Yves Saint-Laurent suit, gray turtleneck, and patent leather shoes, flung open the office door.

The Frenchman was a killer for hire, well known to Tony Bavetta, and held in the highest regard by many of the Mob Bosses in town. His weapon of choice: a Glock 9-mm pistol with silencer. He enjoyed getting up-close and personal when he killed, delighted in the look of terror in his victim's eyes. If they were foolish enough to plead for their lives, it only heightened the man's pleasure, and slowed his target's demise. The man had no sense of loyalty, or affiliations of any kind. He was a loner. He killed, got paid, and moved on. Bavetta didn't entirely trust the Frenchman, nor did he particularly like him, but as a professional killer he was unmatched in the ruthless pursuit of his targets. He never missed, never disappointed. In the company of his peers, Bavetta often opined that the Frenchman was the most elegant, well-mannered, cold-blooded psychopath he ever met. That statement always elicited belly laughs accompanied by nods of agreement.

"*Allo, Monsieur* Bavetta. I trust you are good, no?" the Frenchman said, sauntering up to the desk.

"Am I good? No. That's why I asked for you. I want you to continue shadowing Trey Laughlin. It tears at my gut, but I need to know if I can trust him. Lately he's been," he paused, "off."

"Ah, I see. May I?" The Frenchman gestured toward the guest chair.

"No." Bavetta enjoyed the Frenchman's look of indignation. "I've given him a very important job. He mustn't fail. If something does go wrong, follow these instructions." He slid the note across the desk. "It contains all the information you'll need."

"As always, *Monsieur* Bavetta, I will not disappoint." He snapped up the slip of paper. "Until tomorrow, then." The Frenchman flipped a two-fingered salute and left the room.

"I hate it when he does that," Bavetta muttered.

Chapter Six

After leaving Bavetta's office, Trey detoured to the downstairs washroom where, for nearly ten minutes, he alternately splashed cold water on his face and paced anxiously until the knot in his belly loosened. Now, he ambled toward the Vertigo Palace exit, lost in thought.

"Hey there, Big Guy. Can I buy you a beer?" Maggie called out from behind the bar. It was late afternoon, the bar was quiet, and she busied herself with wiping the bar top to a lustrous shine.

Trey turned. "No, I gotta go. Can't talk right now."

"Couldn't talk much before either," she said, grinning. "Come on. Come sit at the bar for a bit. I've got to talk to you. *Please.*" She channeled a pouty little girl voice and jutted her lower lip for effect.

"C'mon, Maggie. You know I can't say no when you do that." Maggie's playfulness always jolted Trey out of any somber mood. "Okay. Just for a minute. Then, I gotta go take care of some business."

"*Business* is what I wanted to talk to you about. I'll get you a beer."

"Jack. Straight up. Make it a double," Trey said, plunking down on a stool. Reticent to meet her gaze, he studied the bar top with the intensity of a pirate contemplating a treasure map.

"Wow, must be a big job." She half-filled a tumbler and slid it over to him. "There you go, one *Big Gulp* of Jack." She hunched over, leaned on the bar, slipped an index finger under his chin, and raised his head until they were eye-to-eye. Softly, she said, "You know, I've been around here for a year now. I've made a lot of friends and I hear things. I know what's going on. Even more than you might think. I know you have a lot of respect for the Boss and I don't want to hurt your feelings. But, Tony Bavetta...well, he gets a piece of you, or anyone for that matter, and it's like you belong to him. You know what I mean? It's like you're becoming his property. Each time you do his bidding, he takes more. Until one day you *are* his property."

"Look—"

"No, please let me finish." A loud clatter erupted from the kitchen and her head whirled in its direction. She nervously scrutinized the bar area and when satisfied they weren't being watched, continued quietly, "I know what the Boss asked you to do. You can't do this. If you do, he'll have that last little piece of you. That piece that still holds a sense of what's right, and what's of value. If you do this, he'll own you, body and soul.

"Whoa, I don't know what you heard, but it's no big deal. I need to do this. It's my job." Unsure of what Maggie may have heard, Trey had no doubt she couldn't possibly know the job's true details. Mister Bavetta was a fiercely secretive man and made it clear to all in his employ that *any* information leak would be punished by death. There were no second chances.

"So, you're telling me it's just an ordinary, run-of-the-mill job," said Maggie, uncertainty splashed across her face.

He swallowed a mouthful of Jack and stole a glance behind her, in the direction of the stairway leading up to Bavetta's office. It suddenly seemed as dark and foreboding as an abandoned mine shaft. "Yeah, same ol', same ol'. Honest." He hated to lie to her but couldn't bear to speak of his assignment: the assignment to kill a man. If she found out, he truly believed her opinion of him would be damaged beyond repair. He didn't want that. Couldn't live with that. Maggie was much too special.

"Hey, it's me here," she said, standing upright and thumping palm to chest. "I'm probably the only true friend you have around this place. Please don't lie to me now. I know Bavetta found out his son is seeing Adalina Pentangelo. I also know he wants you to kill him."

Chapter Seven

Jean-Louis Dupont stood amidst the hustling crush of pedestrians in the shadow of the towering glass and steel facade of the AADCO Building. The steady swish of mid-afternoon traffic, bleating car horns, and burning stench of exhaust fumes, were giving him a headache. He hated big American cities and frequently longed for the beauty of *Marseille*. Work was plentiful here; the money excellent, and he truly loved his job. He was very good at it, too. At twenty-nine, he was considered young to have garnered such an infamous reputation amongst the American mobster population. In Mob circles, he became known as "the Frenchman", and he accepted the moniker with great pride.

He began to walk while he read the slip of paper Bavetta gave him, and huffed disapprovingly. The man wanted his own son dead. *Mon Dieu, what kind of father does that?* A part of him respected Tony Bavetta, yet another abhorred the crass little man who he saw as nothing more than an uncultured hooligan. He certainly did not fear the Mob Boss, for he feared no one. He saw the terror-filled eyes of too many men right before the squeeze of the trigger. Tony Bavetta, when faced with his own mortality, would be no different. He would surely beg, then grovel, and finally, soil himself. In his experience, most men were cowards, even powerful ones. Only honorable men died with dignity, and Tony Bavetta was *not* an honorable man.

He did not consider Bavetta a friend, nor did he particularly want his friendship, and was certain the Mob Boss's feelings were mutual. He was merely a means to an end and represented all things the Frenchman coveted: success, power, and wealth. Bavetta was a man held in the highest regard by his peers. Tales of his meteoric and blood-splattered climb to the top of the Mob ladder endured like a mythical yarn spun throughout time. If he were to have any hopes of reaching such heights in this city, Tony Bavetta would be the man in which to emulate.

First, he had to impress the Mob Boss with his work. So far so good. Second, he needed to secure a position at the man's right hand. His ambition to acquire the enforcer job trumped all else and only one person stood in his way: Trey Laughlin. He likened Laughlin to a big, dumb, farm boy who, if not for sheer happenstance, would never have managed to land the job of his own volition. Although, only a fool would fail to notice the mutual respect and almost familial connection the two men shared. Jean-Louis Dupont was no fool. Therefore, he had to tread lightly. It was a stroke of luck that, of late, Laughlin was scripting his own early retirement by bungling one job after another. In the Mob world, retirement meant death. Perhaps he could help that along.

Tonight, Trey Laughlin had to fail. That would be the *pièce de résistance*. "The final nail in the coffin," as the American's say. He must formulate a plan quickly.

The Frenchman plucked his phone from his pocket and entered the time and location of tonight's rendezvous. He tore up Bavetta's note and tossed the pieces into a nearby storm drain. He needed to remove himself from this insufferable clamor and go someplace quiet to think.

Chapter Eight

Trey's heart lunged at his throat, choking his words. "How could you know that? You shouldn't know such things. That's not cool. It's dangerous, too. Who told you about the Boss's son?"

"I have my sources," said Maggie. "Anyway, it doesn't matter who told me. What matters is that I know the truth. I also know you can't kill anyone. It's just not in you. If you do, you'll never be the same after. I couldn't bear to see that."

"I gotta do this. I got no choice. I screwed up and I need to make it right with the Boss."

"You *do* have a choice." Her tone became urgent. "You could get the hell out of here. Start over somewhere else. Please, Trey, listen to me. You ever been to Rio? Well, I have. It's gorgeous. You could go there, change your name and start over."

"No!" he shouted. He glanced around, but it didn't appear as if he drew anyone's attention. He took her hand, gently, yet firmly, and gazed into her eyes. "You don't understand. Before Mister Bavetta, I was nothin'. I never had anyone. I barely knew my old man. My old lady, well, she was more taken with her boyfriends than with me. That's how I got this." He pointed to his scarred chin.

"What do you mean?"

"I was sixteen, wild, didn't give a shit about no one. Never did so well in school, so I quit. The asshole boyfriend-of-the-week, can't even remember his name now, picked a fight with me right in front of my old lady. He was drunk, wouldn't let up, so I hit him. *Hard.* He pulled a knife and cut me. She did *nothin'.*" Trey's jaw clenched with barely restrained emotion. "Anyway, I made him regret it. Then I left. Never saw them again. After that I just drifted around for ten years. Never could hold a job for long. Only thing I ever had going for me was my size. But no one pays you for that. So, I started stealing just to get by. Then I met Mister Bavetta, and he gave me more than just this job. He gave me a new life."

"I know it must have been hard for you at sixteen, to be cast aside by your parents, to have to live on the street like that. Tony Bavetta didn't *give* you anything. He just *took*. Don't you see that? He took from you what he needed. That's all he ever does. He uses people until they're no longer useful to him. Then..." She trailed off, shook her head, and held her arms up as if in surrender.

Her eyes were pooling now, and seeing that tightened his throat. He continued, softer, "He did give me something. I got some purpose now. I got a family. Mister Bavetta's my family. You're family. If I don't got this," he made a sweeping motion with his hand, "I got nothin', no one." He leaned back and puffed out a breath through pursed lips. "Been in a little slump lately, and I disappointed the Boss. This'll make it right. This'll make everything all right." As he spoke, Maggie's head swiveled back and forth in a succession of no's. He knew she was disappointed in him and afraid for him, and it hurt, bad. There was nothing else to say. "I'm sorry. I know you'll probably hate me. You'll see. It'll be okay."

"It won't be okay." Maggie lapsed into a whisper. "I've seen this guy around lately. He's tall and skinny. Looks like a model for *Men's Fashion Magazine*. There's something about him. He scares me. I've seen him going into Bavetta's office, and then soon enough, he starts strutting around the club like he owns it. I don't like it one bit. Please, you can't do this."

"The Boss has a lot of friends. It's probably nothing. Look, I really gotta go. I got some stuff to do." He rose from his stool, flashing a look of determination.

She straightened up, parted her lips as if to speak, and then clamped them shut.

Trey paused at the door, turned. "I'll see you later, Maggie. Don't worry, I got everything under control."

KNUCKLING AWAY A STRAY tear, Maggie watched Trey leave.

She crouched behind the bar, found her purse, dug out her smartphone and shakily scrolled through the contact list.

"There," she said, finding what she was looking for. She touched the screen, pressed the phone to her ear, and waited, fidgeting anxiously. "Hey, Bennie. It's me. I need your help. There's a little task I'd like you to do." She turned and peered through the large, plate-glass window to the east. The wind-driven rain speckled the glass, distorting the panorama of the sprawling city, as if viewed through tear-washed eyes. Though she was inside and warm, Maggie shivered.

Chapter Nine

Crowbar in hand, Trey slipped into the warehouse through an obscure doorway lit only by the parking lot's distant lights. Mister Bavetta's note informed him that the door would be unlocked, which it was. It also revealed that Marco Bavetta was instructed to use the very same entry point and security would not be an issue. His first priority: survey the immediate surroundings and carefully search for an ambush spot. Ideally, he had to be out of sight, and most importantly, positioned so that Marco Bavetta – to call him a deadbeat just seemed wrong – would pass right by him.

It was 9:42 p.m. and the massive warehouse had emptied of workers hours ago. If it weren't for the squealing of rats, it would be quiet. Personally, he preferred the quiet. He tried his best to ignore the scurrying creatures and plodded forward. Tonight, rats were the least of his concerns.

With the outside light extinguished by the closed door, the narrow entryway was cast in darkness. Trey held the crowbar chest high as he shuffled along, groping the wall with his free hand, waiting for his eyes to adjust. The air was dank, stale, and smelled of engine grease and diesel fuel.

After twelve feet, the hall spilled out into the open expanse of the warehouse. High overhead, the lackluster glow of a scant few security lights struggled to illuminate the sizable interior. Trey strained to see into the gloom. He shrugged. The deep shadows and murky lighting would be to his advantage. Multiple rows of shelving bays tunneled away until they disappeared into black at the far end of the cavernous room. The bays to his left were empty. To his right, they were stuffed with boxes and shipping crates. Trey could only imagine what they contained – or concealed. Under the guise of Plato International Shipping and Transfer, Tony Bavetta imported a variety of items, but weapons and drugs usually filled the manifest. Not that they were listed as such. The contraband would be hidden inside household appliances, furniture, televisions, and as far as Trey knew, even in sacks of coffee beans and grain.

He continued to hunt for a place to hide. As he examined the surroundings, he thought of Maggie. Her face plagued his thoughts. The sadness, disappointment, and most of all, the fear in her eyes stung his conscience and riddled him with guilt. *Why did she have to find out about the job?* So much unnecessary pain and worry could have been avoided. He never delved deeply into his feelings for Maggie, but it was fast becoming obvious she held a precious place in his heart. So precious, perhaps, that he locked the feelings away out of fear he'd be left vulnerable to hurt.

He was overcome by a strong need to call her, to tell her everything would turn out fine, to tell her he was sorry. He couldn't though, even if he wanted to. He took no chances and stowed the phone in the glove compartment of his truck, which was parked on a dark side street some three blocks away. He couldn't mess up this job and those damn phone calls had interrupted him for the last time. After all, the Boss told him to call *after* completing the job. When it was all over, it would only take a few minutes to walk back to the truck.

After the initial sweep, Trey decided that the best plan was the simplest plan, so he hid around the corner at the end of the dark entryway. He made sure his shadow was not visible and his reflection could not be seen on any distant surface, and settled in.

Damn near perfect, he thought. From here, he would hear the door open, see the pale glow of the parking lot lights and know exactly when Marco entered. He squeezed the crowbar, feeling the cold metal in his palm. Usually, at moments such as this, calmness settled in, but not on this night. Marco Bavetta was the son of his employer, and definitely not a deadbeat. Yet, he would receive the ultimate beating, one that would end his life. *Because of what, bangin' some chick?* In Trey's assessment, the punishment didn't fit the crime.

"You can do this, Trey. You gotta do this," he muttered in the near dark.

Trey's stomach tightened at the prospect of committing murder, and his conscience struggled to come to terms with it. Persistent memories of Maggie's anguished face and her harsh criticism of the Boss clouded his thoughts and added to his turmoil. His throat was dry and he couldn't seem to steady his staccato heartbeat.

"C'mon, Trey. Get a grip. It's gonna be over soon." The self-directed pep talk had the desired effect and his shaky nerves began to settle, until the door handle rattled and a shockwave of anxiety rippled through him.

WHILE TREY SCOURED the warehouse for a hiding place, the Frenchman waited in his rented, black Peugeot just outside the warehouse lot. He pulled far enough off the darkened roadway to easily go unnoticed by any passing car, most specifically, Marco Bavetta's. He cracked open the window so he could hear the car as it drew near. He then busied himself with loading cartridges into the magazine of the Glock, fourteen in all. Not that he would need that many, but it was prudent to be prepared. He slid the magazine into the gun, eased back the slide until it clicked, extended his arm and tested the sights.

"*Magnifique,*" he uttered.

He ached to squeeze the trigger, but that would come soon enough. He removed the silencer from the case on the car seat beside him and slowly, methodically, twisted it onto the muzzle, savoring every rotation.

Headlights carving through the darkness and the crunch of gravel under tires alerted him to an approaching vehicle. He slid down in the seat, only peeking over the dashboard when certain the vehicle had passed. A white SUV maneuvered through the lot and lurched to a stop at the east side of the building.

Overhead, a seagull shrieked. The Frenchman inhaled the scent of sea air. To him, it smelled foul, like raw sewage, reminding him of the rotting stench of death long after the fun of the kill. He'd rather not think of death in such negative terms though. For it was a beautiful thing. Death was inevitable, and the acceptance of that reality could only result in an honorable death. He planned to die that way, holding his head high, smiling in the face of his demise. Until that time, he had many goals to accomplish and much life to live.

He stroked the barrel of the Glock, waiting, watching, as the young man sprang from the car and disappeared into the shadows of the building.

It was 9:57 p.m.

Time to make his move.

Chapter Ten

Trey pressed his back to the wall as the entryway flooded with muted light. Marco Bavetta had arrived. He squeezed the crowbar and took a long, silent breath.

Soft footfalls crept along the concrete floor, drawing nearer, growing louder. Grasping the crowbar by the chisel end, he raised the clawed hook to ear level. Keeping his back to the wall, he shuffled to the corner. Marco was very close now.

When a cell phone rang, Trey's knees went weak and every nerve ending in his body screamed. His mind whirled. He was certain he left the phone in the truck. Was he going crazy?

Then, an uncertain, "Hello...?"

Relief washed over Trey at hearing Marco's greeting.

"Who is this?" Marco continued in a whisper. "What?"

Silence.

"Is this some kind of a joke? That can't be true." The young voice cracked, fraught with urgency and alarm. "Yes. I see. All right."

Trey wanted to pounce and take a mighty swing with the crowbar, but he didn't move, *couldn't* move.

The conversation halted. Trey strained to listen, but heard only the squealing of rats. Then, barely audible, yet unmistakable, the soft rustling of cloth caught his attention. *What's he doing now?*

What he heard next changed everything.

A metallic click.

A sound he knew all too well. In this business, you had to know it: the hammer of a revolver pulling back, locking into place. Probably one of those flimsy .38 Specials, Trey imagined; flimsy maybe, but lethal, especially in close quarters.

"Where are you?" the young voice quivered. "I know you're here. I've got a gun. Show yourself."

Shit! Someone tipped him off. Be cool. Just be cool. Suddenly, in the face of this unexpected development, a deep calm settled over him. There was no time to think about who ratted him out. With hiding no longer an option, he had to act. Trey slid the crowbar into the back of his pants, raised his arms, and took one long, slow stride out into the open.

He and Marco were now standing six feet apart. In the grayness, he could see Marco's eyes gaping up at him, could clearly see the extended arm with gun in hand. The other held the phone, which remained at Marco's ear.

"Hey, I know you. You work for my father. You're the bouncer." Marco glanced at his phone, incredulous, as if it was the instrument through which a deep secret was revealed.

"Look, kid..." Trey stepped forward.

"No! Get back! Over there." He waved the gun, gesturing for Trey to back up. "Out in the open. I want to see you."

The gun, cocked and ready to fire, trembled in the younger Bavetta's hand, so Trey obliged. He was now fully exposed. Here, he was vulnerable. The kid was smart.

"Okay. Stop right there," Marco said, advancing cautiously. When he stepped into stronger light, Trey was struck by how much the son resembled the father. He came up just shy of average height, had a stocky build, and possessed a thicker growth of his father's ebony hair, but his youthful face had softer edges, kinder features. This was *not* the face of a killer.

"Just relax, kid. I can explain everything." Trey needed a distraction, but first, he needed to settle Marco down. His trigger finger looked tense. *Way* too tense.

"Where's my father?" The phone crackled and hissed. "Wait." Marco listened intently to the unknown snitch. He glared up at Trey, seemingly aghast at what he was hearing. "No. You're lying! I don't believe you! He would never do that. He couldn't. Not to me, his own son. Not even that son-of-a-bitch would do that!"

Although words weren't Trey's strong suit, he had to say something. The kid was getting too wound up. "I don't know who you're talking to Marco, but he's playing with you." He had to assume that Marco was now being let in on the plan. Even though Trey barely knew his own old man, and still despised him for abandoning him and his mother, he couldn't imagine being told your father wanted you dead. That had to hurt, and hurt bad. It might also provide a much-needed distraction.

THE FRENCHMAN HUDDLED behind a small utility shack, some thirty feet from Marco's unoccupied SUV. The jaunt from his car to the warehouse took longer than estimated and he seethed with anger at his miscalculation. Too much time was lost and Marco Bavetta was already inside with Laughlin. He had to move fast, but with caution.

Marco would be the first target. He had to kill the youngster before Laughlin got the chance. Then he'd call Bavetta and report that his enforcer failed once again. The Mob Boss would most certainly become enraged.

Bavetta's scrawled instructions were quite clear in the event of Laughlin's failure: *Kill my son. Report back immediately for further orders.*

Although the note made no mention of it, he knew Bavetta would have no choice but to order Laughlin killed as well. The man would need to save face or risk the appearance of weakness in the eyes of the Mob's upper echelon.

Bavetta's note revealed that Laughlin was armed with a crowbar and nothing else. The Frenchman patted the breast pocket of his coat and felt the solid resistance of the holstered pistol underneath.

Laughlin's pathetic choice of weapon will be his downfall.

Hunching, he sprinted from the dark nook and crouched behind Marco's vehicle. From this vantage point he could clearly see the closed warehouse door.

I must hurry.

A gust of sea-chilled wind slashed through the night like a scythe, nipping at the exposed skin of his neck and face. He flipped his collar up against the bitter edge of it, withdrew the Glock, and dashed toward the door.

Chapter Eleven

The kid was crying now. Despite efforts to stifle the tears, his brown eyes glistened. His phone hand dangled limply at his side, as if the weight of the snitch's disclosure transformed the device to lead.

"My father hired you to kill me? Why?" Marco spouted, eyes burning up at Trey.

Trey grew used to seeing fear in his target's eyes, but this was *pain*. Not the kind he usually inflicted. This was pain of the heart, and it seemed bottomless. "You disappointed your old man. He didn't wanna have to do this, but you hurt him. Hurt him bad. That made him real mad. He heard about the girl. You had to know he would find out." *I gotta get the gun away from the kid.*

"You mean about Addy? What about her?"

"You had to know she's Dino Pentangelo's kid. Your old man and Pentangelo, they hate each other. Have for years." *Time to make my move, ever so carefully, for the crowbar.*

"We love each other. I don't care about that stuff. I don't ever want to be involved in my father's business. Addy, well, she feels the same way about her father. We don't care about their stupid feud. We want to get married. Get out of this town, this country." The gun, still pointed at Trey's head, shook with increased fervor. Marco, inching forward, said, "My father never gave a shit about me. He cares only for money, for power. So why should I give a shit about what hurts him? You tell me that. Why?" He continued to advance, narrowing the gap between them, now within the big man's reach.

Their eyes were locked. Trey slowly reached behind and felt the cold comfort of steel. He suddenly caught a glimpse of something in the corridor, just behind Marco's head; a soft glow. *Was that there before?* His eyes shifted to Marco, and then flitted back to the now darkened corridor. Trey wondered if his eyes were playing tricks on him.

"What are you looking at?" Marco asked.

"Nothin'." He could work with this. Make Marco think there was something behind him. The oldest trick in the book, sure, but the kid was jumpy, and maybe naive enough to buy it.

The door latch clicked.

Marco's brow furrowed. He glanced over his shoulder.

Trey extracted the crowbar with quick-draw speed and in one fluid motion lashed out at the gun, hitting the target dead on.

Marco yelped in shock and pain. The gun clattered to the floor. Marco lunged for it. Trey, having superior reach, kicked at it, knocking it away from the young man's grasp. It slid easily on the painted concrete floor and disappeared under a forklift.

Marco paused, craned his head up at Trey, and then slowly righted himself.

Trey towered over him in the gloom, crowbar at his side, ready to strike. There was a searing intensity in the kid's eyes, a resolve. He didn't whimper, didn't scream or beg. Didn't even try to run. *The kid has guts. I gotta give him that.*

"You going to kill me now? Is that what my father *uses* you for, to do his dirty work? Well, you must be very proud. I'm sure he'll give you a big promotion with more money, more power. That's what you really want, isn't it? I'm just a means to an end, aren't I?"

Trey's roller coaster thoughts turned to Maggie. He rubbed a hand over his face in an attempt to clear his head. *Dammit Trey, focus! You can do this. It's what Mister Bavetta wants and you owe him so much.* Yet, a single overpowering emotion tugged at him: doubt. So many questions sprouted in his mind.

"Why didn't you just run? I mean before, when you got the call. When you were tipped off. You could have run away then." *It's not time for talk, Trey. Get on with it.*

"I-I don't know. I guess I didn't believe it. I wanted to see for myself, wanted to believe it was my father standing where you were. That maybe he really planned to make things right with me. Guess I got my answer..." Marco's voice choked off.

"So, who were you talking to?"

"Why all the questions? Why don't you just kill me and get it over with?" Marco remained surprisingly defiant, stubbornly standing his ground.

The nagging possibility of a connection to his own mystery caller urged Trey on. "I gotta know who called."

"Jesus, I don't know! I didn't recognize the voice. It was garbled, distorted. Anyway, why should I care? It's too late for me now. If you're going to kill me, just do it. Do it!" His jaw went taut, his eyes fixed and fiery.

Yeah. Just do it. Just whack the kid. Put us both outta our misery. "I'm sorry, but I got no choice." He hefted the crowbar high above his head. It never felt heavier.

Marco squeezed his eyes shut and turned his head away, breathing rapidly and trembling uncontrollably.

The kid looked so helpless, so small, yet acted like the biggest man Trey ever encountered. In the face of death, the kid showed dignity, and strength. Trey wondered if he could say the same for himself. Could he? Was Mister Bavetta taking it all from him: his dignity, his sense of honor? Had the line between wrong and right become so blurred he no longer knew the difference? Maybe Maggie was right.

Trey expelled a long breath, and slowly lowered the steel bar. "Hey, kid. Get lost. Go on. Get outta here. You better go fast and you better get as far away from here as possible. *Now!*"

Marco forced open his eyes and stared up at the big man. At first, Marco looked dubious and inched backward. Then he spun around and darted toward the exit, disappearing around the corner.

Unexpectedly, Trey heard Marco scream in terror. "What the hell? Who are you? No, please!" The young man's sudden outburst shot from the corridor like a cannon blast, prompting Trey to take a tentative step in that direction.

Before Trey could take a second step, he heard the ping-ping of two silenced gunshots.

He watched helplessly as Marco Bavetta staggered back into the somber light of the open area, forehead bleeding from two dime-sized holes. Marco's lifeless body crumpled to the floor some six feet from where Trey stood frozen in shock and horror.

Chapter Twelve

Vertigo Palace roared as the sardine-thick crowd enjoyed thundering music and soaked up an endless flow of cocktails and beer. A band was performing on the stage and, in an unusual change of pace, rock and roll music ruled the night. A throng of gyrating bodies bounced on the dance floor to a Rolling Stones cover band, a long-standing favorite of Tony Bavetta's. A stack of Marshall Amps pounded out the boisterous music as the lead singer strutted around the stage like a wild turkey in heat.

Pleased to meet you
Hope you guess my name
Ooo, who...Ooo, who

Bavetta lounged in his box seat, accompanied by friends, fellow gangsters, and two men built like lumberjacks, his personal security detail, Manny and Jake. Normally, Trey Laughlin would be at his side on nights such as this, but the big guy had more important things to do. Bavetta paid little attention to the people surrounding him. The buzz of their conversation and the pitch of their laughter simply blended with the ambient racket. Instead, he stared steadfastly at the stage, his face bereft of expression, his body unmoving except for one hand, which distractedly swirled a Glenfiddich on the rocks.

But what's puzzling you
Is the nature of my game

Ooo, who…Ooo, who

In addition to tending bar, Maggie Valente, at his request, also worked his personal box on this particular night. "Another Scotch, Mister Bavetta?" she asked flatly, approaching the table.

"My dear Maggie, how many times have I told you to call me Tony? A hundred, a thousand?" He grabbed her hand.

"Sorry, I guess with you being my boss and all, it makes me uncomfortable. I was raised to respect authority. It's just a habit. Nothing personal." Maggie gazed nervously down at the Mob Boss and then at their intertwined hands.

"You know, I like you Maggie. Always have. Why, I'd even say that you're like family to me." Her hand tensed, as if his touch repulsed her. He didn't like that at all and tightened his grip, tugging her closer. "Is there something I should know about? Tonight, you seem…distracted. Anything on your mind?" He flashed a shrewd smile.

"No. I'm fine. It's just that Trey is usually here on nights like this and I guess I miss him."

Bavetta's eyes turned cold. "He's working. He can certainly take care of himself. He's got his work to do, and you've got yours. So you see there's no reason for a barmaid to worry over one of my boys." He felt an odd pang of jealousy, but suspicion and doubt overshadowed it. This evening, he caught Maggie on numerous occasions glancing surreptitiously over at him as one would contemplate a freak at a sideshow, curious yet afraid to make eye contact.

"So, can I get you another drink then, *Tony*?"

She smiled at him, but it seemed strained and insincere. "Another Scotch would be great. Oh, and Maggie, fetch another round for my friends." The Frenchman reported to him that she and Laughlin were getting cozy, maybe *too* cozy. He was also made aware she was snooping around, asking questions. If she stuck her nose where it didn't belong, something would soon have to be done about that. Perhaps the lovely Maggie Valente had overstayed her welcome. He squeezed her hand harder still and returned a wooden smile.

Maggie grimaced and tugged her hand away. "Sure thing. Another round coming right up," she said, turning away.

"Wait, there's one more thing–" The cell phone on the table sprang to life, interrupting him in mid-sentence. Maggie flinched, cocked her head, and eyed the phone anxiously. He locked eyes with her, allowing the phone to ring four times before releasing his gaze and picking it up. "Bavetta," he greeted, waving dismissively to the barmaid.

Maggie hurried off.

"I don't want to have this conversation here. Let me go to my office." When Bavetta's security detail began to follow, he raised his free hand. "It's private business. I'll be fine."

Once inside the office, he shut the door, attempted to engage the deadbolt, but it wouldn't budge. He cursed under his breath and made a mental note to have it fixed. He thought better of flipping on the lights, walked around the desk, and settled comfortably into his chair. "So, am I to assume you are calling because Trey Laughlin has failed?" He plucked a fresh cigar from the box, "I see. That's disappointing. What about my son?" clipped the end of it, "Well, at least that's good news," and lit it, puffing out billows of smoke. "Where are you now?" blue-gray smoke swirled around him, "Then, may I suggest you get back inside and kill Trey Laughlin. When it's done, clean up the mess and get out of there."

Bavetta ended the call and reclined in the chair, Cuban cigar and dark eyes burning. Anger seethed within him, slowly building like steam in a pressure cooker, until he could no longer contain it.

"Dammit!" He tossed the phone across the room, hearing it crash against the wall.

THE FRENCHMAN FUMED, having been at the receiving end of an abruptly halted, and rather unsatisfying, phone conversation. He hated the way Tony Bavetta treated him, the way he smugly dismissed his earlier request to use the guest chair, the way he curtly ended the call in which he announced success while Laughlin continued to fail. He was beginning to feel unappreciated. Things were going to change. Tony Bavetta *will* learn to appreciate him. Tired of drifting around the country, he planned to finally settle down. He was certain his success tonight would result in a position at the Mob Boss's right hand. Had he not repeatedly proven himself to be the best? He had! He *was!*

As Bavetta so succinctly put it, time to go back inside and finish the job. He powered off the phone and dropped it into the hip pocket of his leather jacket. The brisk night air seeped through his gloves and his fingertips tingled. He rubbed his hands together to warm them before removing the Glock from the holster. He eased open the door, and with the stealth of a fox entering a hen house, slipped inside.

Chapter Thirteen

Marco's corpse stared up at Trey with the unseeing eyes of a doll. His conscience pulled him toward the young man's body, but without the luxury of time or the safety of concealment, he had no choice but to leave Marco where he lay. A killer was here, probably hired by the Boss, and Marco Bavetta would not be the only target.

Trey tore his gaze away and scanned the surroundings. He couldn't leave the same way he came in. It would be suicidal. A crowbar against a gun was not a fight he could win. He would have to find another exit, or at least a place to hide. Either way, he needed to act now. Trey sprinted down the nearest aisle, between the towering bays, and into the sheltering gloom.

Something scuffled near the exit, a sound much too loud to be scurrying rats. He quickly ducked between two adjacent bays, wedging his bulk into the slender gap. His keen ears perked. *Footsteps!* They were closing in. It wasn't safe here. He was too vulnerable. He could barely move let alone swing a crowbar. A quick peek around the corner to verify the aisle was empty, and he jogged off again. He moved silently over the concrete floor, using a shuffle-step to mask his footfalls.

Over there! Up ahead to the right. That might work. Where one bay stopped and another began, a sizable cavity came into view. He slipped into the dark nook. Here, there was ample room to move and he was completely surrounded on three sides by bays to the left and right, and a stack of skids behind. He planted the crowbar firmly against his chest, holding it vertically so as not to catch it on the bay's metal edge. The faintest sound would alert his pursuer to his whereabouts.

The warehouse was quiet; too quiet. Even the rats ceased their incessant shrieking. More than anything else, *that* unnerved him most. He took deep, rhythmic gulps of air, steadying his heartbeat and slowing his breathing. A trick he perfected while hiding in dark alleys. Only then, he was the hunter. Now, he was the hunted.

Trey strained to listen. *Nothing, dammit! Where is he? What's he doing?*

When a cell phone's peal shattered the vacuous silence, Trey's heart skipped a beat and his mind went numb. At first, the incessant ringing sounded far away, a distant disturbance, possibly coming from his pursuer. Then it grew increasingly intense, a clangorous poltergeist swooping ever closer. Incredulous, he now realized the racket emanated from the hip pocket of his coat.

"Shit," he rasped through clenched teeth. He fumbled around, feeling the rectangular object's dull vibration as he took hold. He yanked it out and stared at the phone. Not just any phone, but the very same device given to him by Mister Bavetta. The phone he knew, beyond any doubt, should be locked away in his truck some three blocks away. Despite anxious fingers tripping over one another, he managed to power it off. Silence descended like the eerie calm of a hurricane's eye. *What's going on? Am I going crazy?*

Rapid-fire footsteps swept past from the aisle behind him. *No time to ponder. I've got to get outta here now.* Trey darted away.

A millisecond later, two bullets ricocheted off the skids behind him, splintering wood and spraying shrapnel, luckily missing him.

Fueled by adrenaline, he rocketed down the aisle, sneaking a glance back in the direction of the footfalls. Silhouetted feet appeared under the bay at the end of the aisle, some thirty feet away. The hit man would soon round the corner. The next intersection was near, maybe ten feet. He accelerated, and hunched over, attempting to make a smaller target of himself. When he arrived at the intersection, a bullet sparked off a steel vertical support well below his waist.

Careening sharply to the right, stumbling forward, nearly falling, he ran past the first row, racing to the next. Another bullet whizzed by. It missed low, between his legs. He swung right, dashing down yet another shadowy aisle.

A shrill reminder of the phone's presence rocked him again when the announcement of an incoming call pierced the silence. He was so focused on flight he forgot it was in his hand. He catapulted the phone over his head. As it arched over the bay to his right, it went silent before clattering to the floor in the adjacent aisle.

He slipped into a dark sleeve between bays to catch his breath and steady himself. Wedged between well-stocked bays, he readied the crowbar.

Stuttered footsteps resonated from the far end of the aisle, scratching along the coarse concrete floor, suddenly halting. Quiet descended on the warehouse once again. His own labored breathing roared like a wind tunnel inside his skull.

The footsteps resumed, approaching slowly. He was trapped. Time was running out. Options were few. The soft strides stopped.

I'm a sitting duck here.

He could think of only one-way out; wage a surprise offensive attack. Trey squatted as low as he could in the confined space, hoping to catch his pursuer momentarily off-guard. Just one swing of the crowbar, that's all he'd have. The knees would be his target. The pain would be excruciating, taking the gunman down. Fueled by this new hope, his mind and body began to settle into a state of calm.

That is, until, a muffled ring-tone chimed from within his coat pocket.

Chapter Fourteen

"**H**ey, Sandy," Maggie yelled over the din to the blonde-haired server. "Would you mind taking care of the bar for a few minutes? I need to powder my nose."

"Sure thing," the young waitress beamed.

Maggie nodded, grabbed her purse from under the bar, and proceeded to the rear of the club. She stopped at an entryway where one stairwell descended to the "Employees Only" washrooms and the other ascended to Bavetta's office. She glanced back toward the box area. The bodyguards faced away from her, preoccupied with the band. *Jumpin' Jack Flash* boomed throughout the club. *Tonight*, thought Maggie, *is one of the loudest at Vertigo Palace by far.* Perfect for her plan. She couldn't believe her luck when a few minutes earlier she saw Bavetta head upstairs unaccompanied by his two goons. She knew right then she had to act quickly.

Maggie crept up the stairs on shaky legs, her heart rate climbing with each step. She halted at the top and took one last look down the darkened stairwell. No one followed her. *Good.* Even if Bavetta saw her leave the bar through his two-way mirror, he would most likely assume she was heading to the facilities.

Maggie planted her back against the wall to the right of the office door. The small foyer, barely illuminated by a jaundiced overhead bulb, would provide the cover she needed to prepare herself. She dug into her purse, retrieved the .38 and released the safety. She then lowered her purse to the floor, freeing her hands for the task at hand.

She knew Bavetta always locked his door, but came prepared for that. Earlier, she hid two pins in her flowing hair. While living in Canada, she became quite adept at lock picking. A skill she executed with utmost precision during her cat burglary days. That seemed so long ago now. Another lifetime.

She decided to try the door first. She gingerly grasped the doorknob and gave it a snail-slow turn. She felt the door separate from the jamb. *Unlocked! What a break.* The stars were magically aligning for her tonight. She took a deep breath, thumbed back the hammer of the revolver, shoved open the door, and sprang inside.

Chapter Fifteen

Like a plague, terror spread through Trey's body and mind as he fumbled for the phone. He stared in disbelief at the very same phone he tossed away only seconds earlier. He did, didn't he? The approaching jeopardy was now completely forgotten and he slowly raised himself up.

This can't be happening!

Had he been transported into a nightmare? A bizarre dream world where the impossible becomes possible, the unreal, real? Reason began to slip away as he gaped at the ringing phone.

Two words blinked up at him from the tiny screen: Incoming call... Incoming call... Incoming call... flashing repeatedly, burning hypnotically into his brain. His jaw slackened. His eyes glazed. The number that appeared under the two mesmerizing words came as no surprise: 616-565-7734.

He became vaguely aware of a tapping sound somewhere off in the distance. Then again, maybe it was nearby. He couldn't tell, couldn't focus. The tiny screen glowed algae-green in the darkness, drawing him further inward.

Uncontrollable tremors struck his hands, blurring the numbers on the screen, making it increasingly difficult to maintain a grip. Finally, the phone slipped through trembling fingers and plummeted floor-ward. He swiped at it with his left hand, caught it, and fumbled it, desperately trying to regain a hold. Every movement seemed deliberate, like a movie action sequence slowed for effect.

Finally, he managed to squeeze the phone between thumb and fingers, a tenuous grip at best. The phone was now upside-down in his hand, his thumb partially obscuring the number. At that moment, with the persistent ringing assaulting his eardrums, the last four digits of the phone number caught his attention.

7734

The four *inverted* numbers blazed up at him. In his mind's eye, each number morphed into a letter until a single word was formed; the mystery caller's origin now revealed.

He couldn't believe what he was seeing. Yet, in Trey's delusional state, it made sense. In some absurdly surreal way, it made sense!

"Hell..." Trey whispered, as if venturing a guess to a difficult question. He righted the phone and stared at the display. "It can't be. Can it?" Could the mystery calls actually come from the flaming bowels of Hell? Could a demon possess a phone? "That's gotta be it," he muttered. "Nothin' else makes sense."

What other possible explanation could there be for such bizarreness? Insanity? It was less terrifying to believe the unbelievable than that. He didn't *feel* insane. If he was caught up in some sort of horrific nightmare, why him and to what end?

Trey teetered dangerously on a tightrope of intense emotions: self-doubt, fear, and panic. He was terrified his mind might snap with the sum of them pushing upon his raw nerves. The part of him that still clung to reality knew danger approached. Yet, as if manipulated by some overpowering force, he felt compelled to accept the call and bring the phone to his ear.

"You have company. Deliver him to me. Kill him." The serpentine voice hissed inside his head, slithering into the deepest crevices of his brain. Background static buzzed with a cacophony of mournful screams, unrelenting wails, and woeful moans. The eerie voice and hideous choir chipped away at his tenuous grip on reality, threatening to plunge him into a quagmire of madness from which there would be no escape.

When a spectral shadow stretched into his periphery, it jolted him back. Now another voice joined the chorus, this one, directly in front of him. "*Monsieur* Laughlin, you are indeed dreadful at hiding, no? I am most certain you could not possibly make any more noise. What kind of fool does not think to turn off his phone when he is working?"

Trey lowered the phone and stared into the muzzle of a handgun. For a number of seconds, the tiny black hole was his sole focus. Gradually, his gaze shifted to the form in the background. The slender man stood with his back to the far bay, just beyond Trey's reach.

"You have made this much too easy for me. I say *merci beaucoup* for that. *Monsieur* Bavetta will be very pleased with me. He will surely make me his new enforcer when I tell him you are dead."

"No..." Everything was getting clearer, the fog lifting, but the disorienting sensation of waking from a nightmare lingered.

Kill him!

"I-I can't..." Trey stammered in response. The voice's origin bewildered him and he glanced down at the cell phone's black screen.

"You can't what?" the hit man asked, arching an eyebrow. "I believe, *monsieur*, you are out of your mind." He leveled the gun at Trey's head, hesitating.

Trey, feeling steadier now, wondered what the shooter could possibly be waiting for. As his head cleared, the gunman's methods started to make sense. First, shooting only at his legs. Then, stalking him until they were face-to-face. Now, with his target trapped and helpless, waiting, as if expecting...*What, for me to beg for my life? When I do, that's when the kill shot will come.* He knew of such men. They lived for the hunt, got off on killing, and enjoyed watching men grovel in the face of death.

Trey thought of Marco Bavetta and stood defiantly tall, his face expressionless.

The air was electric. Seconds ticked.

The gunman frowned. His trigger finger twitched.

Still, Trey showed no crack in his stony facade, reflexively squeezing the crowbar as he braced himself for the flash of the muzzle, the sound of the shot.

Instead of the ping of the silencer, a reverberant ring as deafening as a fire alarm erupted from the gunman's pocket. The startled man recoiled and stared wide-eyed at his target along the pistol's sightline.

Trey on the other hand, having grown accustomed to such disturbances, remained unfazed, using the opportunity to secure a grip on the crowbar.

The rattled man groped for the phone with one hand, while the other squeezed a shot off at Trey's head. It missed its target, embedding deep into the wooden skid behind Trey's left ear.

The ringing soared to ear-splitting levels.

The gunman panicked and stabbed repeatedly at the screen with his thumb, unsuccessfully attempting to power it off. "*Mon dieu!*" With his attention entirely drawn to the phone, the forgotten gun flailed erratically in the other hand.

Trey launched the crowbar like a dagger. The chisel end speared the gunman's chest, splintering a rib and piercing the heart.

An abbreviated gasp gurgled in the stunned man's throat. His body went rigid and his face contorted in agony. For a brief moment, the mortally wounded man fixed Trey with a stare of astonishment. Then his head lolled back and his knees buckled. By the time the Frenchman struck the floor, he was dead.

Chapter Sixteen

"Dammit Manny, I said I didn't want to be disturbed!" Bavetta barked, as Maggie exploded through the door. Thundering music and tepid light from the outer hall spilled into the room. In the dingy light, Maggie could just make out the angry expression on Bavetta's face. "Well then, I guess you're just going to have to suck it up, Buttercup, because I'm not going anywhere." Maggie closed the door behind her, reducing the music to a muffled drone. The ambient glow of the city filtered in through the large window to Bavetta's left, providing sufficient light to illuminate the seated man.

"Who's there?" Bavetta asked, squinting. Anger transformed to alarm when he recognized the shape of a gun in her hand. "What do you want? Wait…Maggie, is that you?"

Maggie took two steps forward. "Not the Maggie you think you know."

"What do you mean? Put the gun down."

"I don't think you're in any position to give me orders. So, if it's all the same to you, I'll keep it right where it is." She paused, scrutinizing the Mob Boss to ensure he possessed no weapon. Both hands were visible. A cigar smoldered in one and the other was curled into a fist on the desktop. Sitting behind the colossal desk, he looked small, not so intimidating. "Perhaps my *real* name will shed some light. You see, I was born Margherita

Pentangelo. Uncle Dino was all I had after you murdered my father."

Bavetta went silent, as if catching his breath. Then said, "That's impossible. I would have known who you were. I would have—"

"You don't know everything. Uncle sent me away when I was a child, up to Canada. You took away my father, and my mother was a useless drug addict, thanks to men like you. Uncle had friends up there and they took care of me, taught me a lot. They even taught me some skills that were somewhat, shall we say, outside the law. Including how to use a handgun. I'm pretty good, too." Maggie cradled her left hand under her right, bracing the revolver.

"Now wait a minute. Let's talk this through. You're obviously not thinking clearly."

"Don't patronize me. There's nothing to talk about. I've – *we've* – waited a long time for this. Twenty years is long enough. That's when you first came to this little paradise, wasn't it?"

"I don't know what you're talking about."

"Oh, but you *do* know. You decided that drugs and guns just weren't lucrative enough for you. So..."

"So *what!*" Bavetta screamed, rocketing from his seat.

"Sit down and shut up!" Maggie trained the gun at Bavetta's head and he sank back into the chair. "I'm talking now. You can't intimidate me any longer. Do you know what I've been through? I was twelve when you killed my father outside of that church. A *church*, for Christ's sake. He died on the steps at my feet." Her voice began to quiver. "And for what? So you could satisfy your thirst for money, for power, and take control of the gambling profits? My family stood in your way, though. All we wanted was what we already had, nothing more. But *you*...you wanted so much more, didn't you? You wanted to be alone at the top of the heap. So you started cutting my family down one by one."

"You seem to have all the gory details, don't you, Miss Pentangelo?" he said, oozing contempt.

"I've had a lot of Google-time on my hands."

"So what are you going to do now that you have my undivided attention?"

"You're done hurting and killing people I love and care for. You think I don't know what you'll do to Trey when he's no longer of use to you? Well, it stops here and now. I can't stand by and watch anymore."

Now that she was here, her target close, her plan approaching fulfillment, she began to waver. *No! I can do this.* It was the only way to avenge her father, to save Trey. Maggie struggled to steady the gun in her hand, but despite her best efforts, small tremors betrayed her.

A smug grin erased the anger from Bavetta's face. "Foolish, foolish girl. Your father died long ago. Killing me won't bring him back. As for your friend, Trey, you're too late." He glanced at his watch. "He's already dead, my dear. There's nothing you can do for him now."

Maggie took a step closer. "No. That's not true!" Bavetta was lying. Trey was alive. She felt it. She couldn't explain why, some manner of intuition perhaps, but she just knew it to be true. Please, God, it had to be true.

Bavetta calmly continued, "You see that roulette wheel over there. It just keeps on spinning, never stops. It gives me comfort because I know that I, too, will never stop. I let people think I had it motorized, but it came to me that way a long time ago. Not from an old rival as I led people to believe. It was, in fact, a gift from a business partner of sorts. Someone with more power than you can imagine."

"So, what's your point? Why are you telling me this?"

"You think you can just bust in here and kill me that easily?"

"That was the plan, yeah."

"That wheel is so much more than a conversation piece. It represents success. *My* success. Look at it. *Look* at it!"

"No." Maggie strained to keep her eyes fixed on Bavetta. She suddenly felt that the very act of gazing upon the wheel would somehow put her in grave danger.

"I even had a dedicated backup generator installed. So, you see, the wheel's power – my power – can't be stopped. Not by someone like you." He reclined in the chair and casually raised the cigar to his lips, puffing hard, exaggerating every movement as if in mockery of her courage. "You don't have the guts to shoot me. You're not the type. Even if you are a Pentangelo," he said, waving the cigar in front of his face.

He looked so sure of himself, the untouchable Mob Boss, the epitome of power, feared by all, sitting behind that big desk, puffing on that disgusting cigar. He made her sick.

When her eyes veered from the cigar, she realized Bavetta's other hand disappeared under the desk. *Damn him, he used the cigar to distract me.* What he couldn't possibly know, earlier she used her lock-picking skills to enter his office. She searched it and discovered the desk's secret compartment. In it, she found a phone and a note, which from reading it, she now knew were in Trey's possession.

Adrenaline bolted through her when she remembered the third object stashed inside.

A Gun!

Bavetta's hand moved with startling speed. Before Maggie could pull off a shot, he was pointing a silver-black object at her.

I was too slow. I'm dead! Maggie reacted instinctively, and squeezed the trigger. The bullet caught him in the center of the chest. Blood spread rapidly outward, an expanding dark stain against his clean white shirt.

Bavetta's eyes, bulging with shock and pain, gawked. Not at her, but at the object in his hand.

Maggie saw that it wasn't a gun after all. It was a phone. *Jesus, it's only a phone. What happened to the gun?* She recalled the unlocked office door, and how unusual it was. Now, there was a phone where a gun should have been. *Karma,* she wondered, *or is there something else at work here?* Mystified, she glared at the bleeding man. The expression on Tony Bavetta's face was a mix of puzzlement and horror. His left hand went limp, dropping the cigar, while the right steadfastly fisted the cell phone as if it burned into his flesh. He shifted his gaze toward her.

Maggie kept the gun trained on the wounded man. She never shot a man before, and as she stared into Bavetta's dark eyes, a cold sweat overtook her, a chill so deep that her teeth chattered and her hands trembled. She felt sick and fought back the acrid taste of bile rising in her throat.

Bavetta slouched forward in the chair. "No. It can't be. Not you...not now." His voice gurgled weakly as blood filled his airways and his life force ebbed like a receding tide. He sagged to the right and tumbled from the chair, disappearing behind the desk.

When Maggie heard the thump, she forced herself to move, and cautiously sidled around the desk. The Mob Boss lay curled in a fetal position, clutching his chest, struggling for air.

Even as death beckoned, Bavetta seethed. "You...bitch. You'll pay for this," he declared between gasps.

"Trust me, after a year in your repulsive employ, I've already paid." Maggie wanted desperately to point the gun at his head, squeeze the trigger and end his miserable life. She just couldn't bring herself to do it. There was enough violence on this night. Tony Bavetta would die alone, bleeding out on his expensive carpet, fighting hopelessly to his last breath. It seemed a fitting end.

Forgetting about the phone clutched in Bavetta's palm, she turned away, approached the two-way mirror, and studied the hard-partying patrons of the club. The bodyguards were still preoccupied with the entertainment. It was time to take her leave of this establishment.

When Maggie returned downstairs she flagged down Sandy, who was animatedly chatting up two young men at the bar.

When the younger woman approached, Maggie shouted over the music, "Hey Sandy. I'm not feeling very well. I think I'm going to call it a night and go home. You mind taking over the bar?"

"Yeah, sure thing. You go on home and take care of yourself. I'll let Mister Bavetta know when I see him."

"Oh, don't worry about telling him. He already knows I'm not myself tonight."

Sandy shrugged and turned her attention to the men at the bar; flirtatiously twirling her blonde locks as she continued to chat.

Maggie snatched her jacket from under the bar and bee-lined for the exit.

Before leaving, she glanced back at Bavetta's office window. The opaque surface reflected the lustrous glow of the nightclub and shimmered like black onyx. The office, originally designed for surveillance, now concealed her secret. Bavetta's tower in the sky, as dizzying as his ego, would be his tomb. Her stomach did a somersault and she quickly turned and hurried to the elevators.

The trip down the elevator and through the lobby went by in a blur. Maggie pushed through the revolving door and strode into the harsh chill of the November night. She tugged her coat tightly around her neck, then sifted through her purse and fished out the cellphone. She had an important call to make.

Chapter Seventeen

For a short while the warehouse seemed as ominously quiet as a mountain cave. Then, gradually, Trey became aware of the rats. Their shrill squeaks grew louder with each passing second, burgeoning rapidly into a nerve-grating peal. What he witnessed next, despite the surreal events of the night, horrified him as no prior event had.

Legions of scurrying vermin streamed toward him from every direction. Along the aisles between bays, over and through racks behind and in front of him, around scattered skids, darting through his legs, and hurdling over his shoulders. He instinctively recoiled in terror, imagining his worst fear to be reality. Trey soon realized the frenzied horde was not intent on attacking him. They were converging on the lifeless body crumpled at his feet. They were feeding now, tearing at clothing, tugging at exposed flesh, surging over the corpse like a swarm of army ants. As they gorged themselves, the clamor was deafening, sickening. In mere seconds, Trey could already see the telltale white of bare bone on the dead man's face. Hollow, black orbs stared up at the horrified man from where eyes and eyelids had once been.

Trey couldn't stomach the grotesque scene any longer. *I've got to get outta here!* He sprang from the nook and barreled down the aisle, stutter stepping around the stampeding creatures, trying to avoid trampling them under foot. The rushing horde paid him no heed as they scrambled toward the corpse, single-minded in their determination to belly up to the macabre buffet.

Finally leaving the rats behind, Trey stumbled along the last ten feet of the aisle, racing toward the exit, where he passed the surprisingly untouched body of Marco Bavetta. The thick shadows of the entryway enveloped him, slowing him down, but he plodded blindly forward. He burst through the door and into the cold night. His chest heaved with the exertion as he puffed out great breaths, which formed vaporous clouds in the frigid night air.

Feeling dizzy and weak, he buckled over, resting hands on knees, trying to calm his labored breathing and thundering heart. Slowly, he recovered his strength and balance. Trey raised himself up, straining to support his substantial frame on wobbly legs.

When the phone in his clenched fist rang, Trey's entire body shuddered. Until now, he completely forgot he still had it with him.

"No! Not again. This shit's gone too far." Furious, he put the phone to his ear, not bothering to check the display. "What do you want from me?" he yelled.

There was a brief silence. Then a soft voice broke in. "Well, that's a fine way to greet me after the day I've had."

Chapter Eighteen

Even as Tony Bavetta's life trickled away, his fury blazed. *That bitch has to die!* He'd see to it! He'd kill the entire Pentangelo family, horribly, mercilessly. He would dance at their funerals, and laugh. Spit on their graves. No, it wasn't going to end this way. He still had strength, still breathed. *I will not die, dammit!* Imaginings of deplorable acts of retribution buoyed his hopes, gave him strength. He tried to raise himself up, only to fail, too weakened by blood loss.

He needed help, but couldn't call out. Choking blood hampered his voice. The music still blared. He could feel the vibrations through the floor. Panic began to claw at his gut.

Then a new hope for rescue quelled the rising panic. *The phone! It's still in my hand, and Manny's downstairs.* Bavetta shakily dialed and put the phone to his ear. Initially, grating static greeted him, and then the phone went dead.

"Come on, come on," he said weakly, strength draining with each passing second.

He tried again. This time, a garbled voice buzzed in his ear, overshadowed by the hiss of interference. "Manny? It's me. I need–" He coughed, spewing droplets of blood onto the carpet. A jolt of intense pain speared through his chest. "Christ, it burns." He clutched his chest and curled into a tight ball. When the pain subsided, he raised the now bloodied phone to his face.

The indiscernible voice endured, resounding like a distant cry over a vast canyon. "Manny..." he rasped; his voice wafer-thin.

The line went dead.

He battled against encroaching darkness, but managed to dial 911. Before the connection took hold, the phone started to ring. *Thank God*, he thought, hefting the phone to his lips. "Manny, please...help me."

"No." A wispy voice, like wind whispering through the boughs of lofty trees, drew out the single word for a ten-count. Once again, the line disconnected.

With the strength of a man stubbornly clinging to the belief he couldn't possibly be dying, that death simply was not an option, he called 911 again. The line didn't engage. Instead, the cellphone erupted into a clamorous knell. In desperation, he pleaded, "Help...*please*..."

"Your soul is mine." The demonic voice echoed inside Bavetta's head, each eerie repetition overlapping the other, melting away what little essence lingered within his mind and body.

"No. It can't be. It's too soon." Despite the hot pain in his chest, he suddenly felt cold, a bone-chilling cold. Terrified, he tried to end the call. It was to no avail. The connection would not sever. The haunting voice would not abate.

As his world tunneled to black, Tony Bavetta stared up in horror at the roulette wheel. It was stone still.

Chapter Nineteen

Maggie's voice was the song of angels, and elation quickly vanquished Trey's agitation. "Maggie, it's you. You don't know how good it is to hear your voice."

"Jesus, Trey. It sure didn't sound like that a second ago."

"I'm sorry I yelled at you," said Trey. "I thought, well, I thought you were someone else."

"Don't worry about it. To be honest, I wasn't sure I'd ever hear your voice again. Bavetta told me you were dead. I had to believe it was a lie. I prayed to God it was a lie. And trust me; I haven't had much luck with answered prayers in my life. You sound like crap. Are you all right?"

"There's just too much to tell right now. I'm okay, but I gotta get out of here first. It's not safe." Trey started walking, taking long strides to widen the gap between him and this nightmare place as quickly as possible. "I screwed up again. I messed up the job and Mister Bavetta found out. He sent a man to kill me. I had no choice. I had to kill him."

"Oh my God..."

"It's all over. I've disappointed the Boss for the last time. There's a contract out on me now and he'll just hire someone else."

"You don't have to worry about *him* anymore. Tony Bavetta is dead."

"*What?*" Rocked by the news, words stuck in Trey's throat. So much had happened. Life would never be the same.

"Trey? You there?" Maggie's anxious voice crackled in his ear.

"Yeah, I'm here. What happened to Mister Bavetta? How do you know he's dead?"

"I know because I killed him."

"Shit, Maggie. You're full of surprises tonight. You gotta know your life is in danger now. You need to get away from here, far away." *So do I,* thought Trey. *To where, though? What do we do now?*

"I had to kill him. I couldn't stand what he was doing to you and," Maggie's voice went silent for a few seconds, "I had to avenge my father. You see...I'm not who you think I am. I'd like to tell you everything because there's so much to tell. I need to say it to your face. We need to meet."

"Where? Can't go home. Mister Bavetta's thugs will be looking for us both now." As he spoke, he exited the parking lot, and noticed a car parked well off the roadway. He stared long and hard at it. The sleek vehicle seemed out of place. He could only assume it belonged to the man he killed.

Maggie's voice turned to a whisper. "The airport. We can meet at the airport. My cousin Bennie's in the travel business and I called him after we last spoke. I have two tickets to Rio, and I'm not afraid to use them. It's the redeye out of this town and into a brand new life, a better life for both of us. Come on, what do you say?"

What do I say? There was no one in the world he would rather be with at this moment. "Maggie, you know I don't speak much, and I never told you, but..." He trailed off, struggling to find the right words.

Maggie's voice cut in, "That's all right. I'll let you off the hook for now. You can tell me later face-to-face. So how does Rio sound? Like you said, we've got to go somewhere far away."

Trey went quiet, his mind a jumble of thoughts.

"Come on, Trey. Don't make me put on my pouty-girl voice."

"You know I can never say no when you do that." The crushing emptiness eased, the weight of the darkness diminishing. Both his spirits and his pace picked up when his black Jimmy appeared in the shadows.

"Great," Maggie said, "I'll take that as a yes. Don't worry about money or anything. I've already taken care of all that with the help of a very dear uncle of mine."

After discussing the details of where and when they would meet up, Trey ended the call.

The Jimmy was parked on a narrow, pot-holed access road, industrial buildings on one side and an eight-foot chain link fence on the other. When he arrived at the truck, he snuck one last look back at the warehouse. From this distance, only a telltale dome of pale light from the parking lot marked its whereabouts. Overhead, ominous clouds of silver-gray swirled on the dark horizon. *Bad weather's coming,* he thought, a cold shiver running through him.

Then thoughts of Maggie warmed him. He was going to Rio with her, leaving this life behind. A few hours earlier, he reacted with stubborn resistance when Maggie proposed he leave this city. The only home he ever knew. Now he felt like he'd been given a second chance, like the puzzle pieces of his broken life were finally fitting together.

He glanced at the phone in his hand. It sparked thoughts of Marco Bavetta and he realized he had one more call to make.

Trey dialed 911 and provided a smattering of information to the calm-voiced woman who answered. After he reported Marco's murder and told of his whereabouts, the 911 operator's tone grew edgy and urgent, her questions becoming more personal and prying. He gave her all the information she needed, and ended the call.

Trey lingered by the driver's door and stared at the blank screen of the cell phone. He no longer had a use for this phone, and right now didn't care to possess one ever again. He hurled the phone as hard as he could, his eyes tracing its flight as it sailed over the fence and out of sight. Hearing it clatter along a hard surface, Trey was overcome by the feeling that the phone would not magically return to his possession as it did before. It was finally over. Somehow, he just knew it. He was too exhausted to question why.

He flung open the Jimmy's door and slid into the driver's seat.

He sat for a moment, clutching the steering wheel, and thinking of Maggie. A smile touched his weary face. He had no idea what he would say to her about the events in the warehouse, or if he would say anything at all. There would be plenty of time to think about that later. He knew the horrific events of this night would eventually fade into the background of his mind, but they would never be forgotten. Even running to another country wouldn't change that fact.

He fired up the engine and put the Jimmy in gear.

In Rio, Trey decided, he would get himself a landline.

Don't miss out!

Visit the website below and you can sign up to receive emails whenever James McHarg publishes a new book. There's no charge and no obligation.

https://books2read.com/r/B-A-IKWC-GWVQC

BOOKS2READ

Connecting independent readers to independent writers.

Also by James McHarg

Emmett Barclay Mystery Series
Sins of the Past
Buried in the Past

Standalone
P3
Incoming Call

Watch for more at https://www.facebook.com/
profile.php?id=100088377614103.

About the Author

James McHarg lives in Ottawa, Canada with his wife. He enjoys spinning dark and mysterious tales of fiction. Initially honing his skills on short stories, he has since published a standalone psychological thriller, *P3,* and the Emmett Barclay Mystery series, *Sins of the Past* and *Buried in the Past*. His thriller, *Incoming Call*, will soon be re-released. Find him on Facebook.

Read more at https://www.facebook.com/profile.php?id=100088377614103.

www.ingramcontent.com/pod-product-compliance
Lightning Source LLC
Chambersburg PA
CBHW020641160726
47991CB00003B/974